The Far, Far Distant Land

Illustrations by Jan Lewis

This book is dedicated to
all children everywhere.

J   F   B   B   G   J   M   S   D   M   C

It was the summer holidays and as usual, the children were travelling on the Cigam Express to stay with their grandparents in the country.

The journey had been long, the sandwiches eaten early on and they were all tired and hungry.

'Are we nearly there?' asked Charlie, for the tenth time. He was the youngest grandchild and all journeys seemed much longer to him than to the others.

'Not far to go now,' said Ben the eldest, looking at his watch. 'It's almost 12.30 and just time to gather up our things'.

The train slowly pulled into the station and the children tumbled out onto the platform.

They stopped short. Instead of Old Joe waiting for them in the wagon pulled by Mabel and Henry, he was in the driving seat of the oldest, strangest bus they had ever seen. Grandad was also there, which was unusual, and he greeted them all with lots of hugs and kisses. In his hands he carried a beautiful model boat.

'When will we play with that?' asked Jake, the second eldest grandchild.

'All in good time,' replied Grandad.

'I'm starving hungry,' said Daisy, and she thought that before long they would be sitting round a table laden with their grandmother's delicious food. But to their surprise Grandad said, 'I've got other plans.'

3

'But when are we going to eat?' asked Daisy.

'Don't you worry about that,' replied Grandad. 'Let's just get you on the bus.'

They threw their luggage in the boot and piled onto the bus. To their delight, on each seat was the largest Cornish Pasty they had ever seen.

Charlie found it too big to hold, so Freya his sister, broke it in half.

'It's got meat and vegetables in one end, and apple and blackberry and custard in the other,' she said.

Sam whispered to Daisy and Bea, 'we can only eat the sweet end. What a pity!'

Grandad overheard, of course, and said, 'Did you think we had forgotten? Of course, yours are without meat .'

'Yummy,' said Mollie the eldest girl. 'I'm going to eat the sweet end first.'

Grandad and Old Joe took their seats in the front and knew they would have a little peace and quiet while the children were eating.

The bus started off and they were on their way.

Sam, who finished eating first, asked, 'Where are we going?'

'Well, I thought we'd go to the Far, Far Distant Land,' said Grandad.

The children cheered.

'You always tell us stories about that,' said Bea, 'but I never imagined we would ever see it. Will it take long to get there?'

'How long is a piece of string?' said Old Joe from the front.

The grandchildren didn't know what he was talking about but were too polite to ask. After what seemed like hours of the bus struggling up and down hills and along the narrow lanes, it began to slow down. The children could see the sea and, before long, the bus drew up to the harbour.

'Out you get!' said Grandad. 'Mind you don't fall in the water Charlie!'

Millie, his older sister, grabbed his hand tightly.

Grandad was still carrying the model boat.

'We need a pond for that, not the sea,' said Joe.

Grandad didn't reply and carried the boat along the jetty and while the children watched, he carefully lowered it into the water, where it bobbed gently in the waves.

'Now for a bit of magic,' he said.

Jake nudged Mollie, they had both been the last to believe in magic and seemed to be up to their old tricks again.

'When I tell you, I want each of you to shut your eyes tight and to turn in a small circle to your right. Then turn very slowly, until I tell you to stop.'

'Which way it right?' asked Daisy.

'You follow the hand you write with, of course,' said George.

'It's called clockwise,' said Ben, who knew longer words than the others.

'Why's that?' asked Bea.

'Because the hands of the clock go to the right,' he replied.

'Let's not waste any more time', said Grandad. 'We'll all have a practice at turning right before the real thing. Ready, steady, go!'

Charlie tried to go left but Millie pulled him to the right.

Daisy also turned left because she wrote with her left hand.

'Other way, Daisy,' whispered Grandad 'the others haven't seen.'

'Right, let's do the real thing now. Don't open your eyes until I tell you, as some of you may be quicker than others.'

Millie kept a hold on Charlie, as Sam helped Joe, who had a poorly leg, and they all turned slowly clockwise.

'Right, open now!' said Grandad.

All eyes opened and the children could not believe what they saw!

The small boat had become a full-sized, rigged sailing boat!

'That is impossible!' said Mollie, 'I can't believe my eyes!'

'That's always been your problem Mollie,' said Ben, her brother. 'How many times do you have to see magic to believe in it?'

'I didn't say I don't believe in magic, I said I didn't believe my eyes!' she mumbled.

'Welcome to the good ship SPELLBOUND,' said Grandad. She will take you to the Far, Far Distant Land. On you go, single file along the jetty and Old Joe and I will help you aboard. Six of you sit on one side and five of you on the other.'

'That's so the weight is not all one side,' said Joe, 'which might make the boat sink.'

'Magic boats don't sink,' said Grandad.

'Off you go now,' he said, when they were all settled on board.

'Aren't you coming with us?' asked Freya.

'No, Old Joe has to work on the farm, and I have to help your grandmother get lunch for you all.'

'We don't know how to get there,' said Millie, nervously.

'The boat knows,' said Grandad 'you just follow the wind.'

And sure enough, the sails filled with wind and the boat slowly left the harbour and out towards the open sea. The figures of Old Joe and Grandad got smaller and smaller and the children were on their way.

Charlie noticed his sailor suit. 'Now we are really ready to sail,' he said.

'What are those silvery, flashes ahead?' asked George.

'I think they are flying fish,' said Jake, who often went fishing with his father.

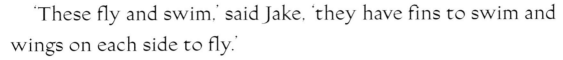

'But fish don't fly,' said Freya, 'they swim!'

'These fly and swim,' said Jake, 'they have fins to swim and wings on each side to fly.'

'Why do they do that?' asked Bea.

'Just for the fun of it,' said Jake.

Before long, the flying fish were dipping in and out of the water alongside the boat, their shiny bodies sparkling in the sunlight. Then, as suddenly as they came, they disappeared and SPELLBOUND carried on its way.

At one point, a large turtle swam up to them and said, in a very turtley voice,

'Would anyone like a lift on my back?'

'Yes please, I'd love to!' said Charlie but Millie gave him a look and said, 'Thank you so much, another time perhaps. We are off to the Far, Far Distant Land and Grandad said we need to stay on the boat until we get there. Are we going in the right direction?'

'Yes, you will soon come to a large rock and might see the lighthouse keeper if you are lucky,' said the turtle.

The children thanked him and they sailed on by.

True enough, before very long they spied a large rock and, as they got nearer, they were amazed to see a dolphin perched upon it carrying a lantern. Even more amazing was that the dolphin was wearing a very frilly skirt!

'That's a tutu!' said Freya, 'I've got one just like that which I wear to ballet!'

The boat slowed down and Joe asked why the keeper had such a large lantern.

'This shows the sailors where the rock is so they know to keep away, for safety', said the dolphin in a gurgly sort of way.

'Excuse me for asking,' said Freya politely, 'but why are you wearing a tutu?'

'I love to dance, of course,' replied the dolphin and he began spinning and leaping around. The children cheered and clapped; it really was the funniest thing they had ever seen.

11

'To tell you the truth,' said the dolphin, 'I'm tired of being a lighthouse keeper and my dream is to be a ballet dancer. Can you arrange that for me?'

'Well, in the magic world, anything can happen,' said Mollie, 'but you must find another lighthouse keeper first to keep all the sailors safe while you are away.'

The dolphin thought for a while then said, 'My friend the octopus would be delighted. He has eight legs and eight lanterns will light up the rock very satisfactorily.'

'What a good idea!' said Mollie. 'The boat will pick you up on the way back from dropping us off in the Far, Far Distant Land. Now, can you tell us the right way to get there?'

'Of course,' said the dolphin. 'Before long you will hear the sound of beautiful singing. Follow the sound and the wind will take you there. And thank you for making my dream possible. But one more thing before you go. Beware of the Evil Sea, which you must cross on the way to the beautiful singing. This sea is beautiful too but is home to sea creatures not as nice as I am. They will try to persuade you to touch them, which is not the best idea in the world.'

'Thank you,' said Joe, 'we must all remember your warning.'

The children waved to the dolphin as the boat sailed on its way. They huddled a little closer together, afraid of what might happen as they crossed the Evil Sea.

Imagine their surprise as SPELLBOUND drew near to an area of colourful shapes moving slowly on the surface of the water.

'This can't be the Evil Sea,' said Sam, 'it is too beautiful.'

'Don't forget we were warned not to touch,' said Millie.

'But look at the smoothness of each one and the lovely colours,' said Daisy.

She painted beautiful pictures and knew all the different coloured paints, and could see the many shades of pink and mauve.

'I think these are jellyfish and I know that many of them could sting us with their tentacles.'

The boat slowed down and a wobbley, jellyishy voice came from just beside the boat.

'Please stroke my balloony back and feel how soft I am.'

'No thank you,' said Jake, who didn't want to upset the jellyfish, 'we really don't want to get our hands wet. I think we will be on our way again. It was very nice meeting you and you certainly are beautiful.'

And the boat sailed on.

Before long, Bea said, 'I can hear the beautiful singing the dolphin told us about', and as they got nearer, they could see another smaller rock.

Swimming slowly around this were three beautiful maidens with long golden hair. The boat drew alongside, and George said, 'Would you like to come aboard for a bit? You must be very tired and we are a long way from land.'

'No thank you,' said one, 'we live in the sea', and with a swish and a slither, she flipped out of the water and onto the rock.

'Good gracious me!' said Freya. 'You've got a fish tail. You're a mermaid. I've heard all about you but never, ever thought I would be lucky enough to see one.'

'Why isn't there a light on this rock?' asked Joe.

'Well, we circle it all the time and sing. Every sailor knows to keep away from singing mermaids!'

'Why is that?' asked Sam.

'Because we try to get them to come down to the bottom of the sea to visit our father, Neptune, the King of the Deep. It's not so nice for them, as they can't live under water. That is why they always sail away if they hear mermaids singing.'

'Well, you do a good job,' said Mollie.

'We do,' said the mermaid 'but we get very tired of doing this all the time and have a dream of singing in a choir, so that the dolphin has music to dance to.'

'How do you know the dolphin?', asked Millie.

'Silly question!' replied the mermaid, rather bad-temperedly. 'We know all the creatures in the sea.'

14

The children thought it was possibly time to go but promised that the boat would be back to pick them up so they could have their dream too.

'But first,' said Joe, 'you must do something to keep the sailors safe from this rock while you are away.'

'That's easy,' said the mermaid, 'our friends the Glowfish shine a beautiful electric green and they can take our place and warn the sailors away. Now I have work to do and cannot stay chatting, so be on your way. There's not far for you to go now. Sail until you meet our other friends, a school of whales.'

'Why do they go to school?' asked Charlie.

'They don't, silly,' said the mermaid, 'a school is the name given to a group of whales.'

'What is a group of mermaids called?' asked Joe.

'A Neptunia of course', she replied, 'now off you go!' And with another swish and a slither, she was back in the water.

SPELLBOUND sailed on and the children amused themselves by seeing how many other groups of names they could think of.

'A heard of cows,' said Freya.

'A flock of sheep,' said Sam.

'A nest of viper,' said Joe.

'A charm of goldfinches,' said Mollie.

'A flutter of butterflies,' said Bea.

'A pod of dolphins,' said George.

'A swarm of bees,' said Daisy.

'A plague of rats,' said Jake.

'A gaggle of geese,' said Millie.

'And a murmuration of starlings,' murmured Ben quietly. He didn't want to show off to the others, even though he was the eldest.

'I don't know any,' said Charlie. 'What about a cousinry of cousins?'

The others laughed and Charlie was happy.

After a while, the boat began to slow down.

'I don't see any land yet, and the wind seems to have dropped,' said Sam.

Sure enough, the sea was calm now and the sails of the boat flapped limply in the breeze.

'How shall we get to the Far, Far Distant Land without the wind in our sails?' asked Joe.

With that, three huge whales leaped out of the sea, with water spurting from their spouts. The boat rocked wildly and the children clung on to the sides.

'Be careful!' shouted George and the leaping stopped as the whales drew alongside.

'How do you blow those lovely fountains of water?' asked Bea.

'Well we breathe through these spouts before diving down to feed. As we come up for another breath, the water spouts out from our airholes.'

'I wish I could do that,' said Charlie.

'Well you don't need to because you don't live under the sea,' replied the whale. 'Now you're going to need our help to get to the Far, Far Distant Land, which is not so far, far distant now. We can blow wind into your sails and get SPELLBOUND on its way.'

'Thank goodness for that,' said Daisy, 'I don't know how we would get any further now the wind has dropped. Shall we get started?'

'Not so fast!' said the whale. 'We are tired of blowing air and water through our spouts all the time, we dream of blowing trumpets instead.'

'Why on earth would you want to do that?' asked Mollie.

'So, we can play music for the mermaids to sing and the dolphins to dance,' said the whale.

'Well, the boat can pick you up on the way back but I suppose you will need someone to do the blowing while you are away,' said Mollie.

'No,' said the whale, we normally swim around the ocean enjoying ourselves but Grandad arranged for us to be here when the wind dropped to help you on your way.'

And with a huge burst of air from their spouts, the sails billowed out again and they were on their way. The whales followed on beside them, each taking a turn in blowing while the others dived down to the seabed.

'I can see land!' shouted George.

And there it was, the Far, Far Distant Land.

'You will just drift into shore now,' said the whale, 'our job is done!'

'Thank you!' they shouted. 'We would never have got here without you!'

18

The children now had a good view of the island. There was a long narrow beach, fringed with coconut trees, behind which were sheer cliffs reaching a wide flat top.

'I don't know how we'll be able to get up there, we're no good at climbing. Apart for trees and wall-bars at school, of course,' said George.

The boat gently made its way to the harbour. There was someone waiting on the jetty to meet them. The boat drew alongside, and Daisy asked in her most polite voice, 'Are you expecting us?'

'Yes, I have waited many years for this,' the man replied. 'I am Professor Spellbinder and, on this island, I teach very special people the art of magic.'

'Does that mean we are very special?' asked Jake.

'Certainly not special in every way but special because you have magic in your family,' the professor replied.

'Do you know our grandad then?' asked Bea.

'Most certainly,' was Professor Spellbinder's answer. 'I taught him magic on this very island, as I taught his grandad before him. And you will need to learn the magic so you will be able to give magical times to your own grandchildren.'

'That's a long way ahead,' said Mollie, 'we are still children ourselves.'

'I know,' said the professor, 'but what you learn today, you will never forget. But you will not have the power to use this magic until you are grandparents yourselves.'

'My parents can't do magic,' said George. The others agreed that their parents were useless at magic too.

'That's because the power misses a generation,' answered the professor.

20

Millie had to explain this to Charlie, as he looked very puzzled.

'I don't learn as quickly as the others,' he said, 'cos I'm the youngest.'

'That will not make a jot of difference,' said the professor, 'you will learn and know all there is to know, exactly the same as your cousins. Now it's time for me to help you ashore,' he said and led them one by one onto the jetty.

The children gazed up at the sheer cliffs facing them. The professor knew what they were thinking and said, 'Do you remember the flutters you had to take you through the magic wood?' The children nodded.

'Well if you look over there, you will see those flutters and they will lift you high above the cliffs and onto the land above.'

And there were the flutters, on the beach at the end of the jetty, and as the children went to put them on Professor Spellbinder took Joe to one side and whispered, 'Your leg is getting better each day and when you put your flutters on you will never ever need to use the crutches again.'

Joe was so happy. 'I will be able to run and jump with the other children now. How are you going to get to the top Professor?' he asked. 'There are no flutters for you.'

'Don't worry about me,' he replied as he helped Joe with his flutters.

Then, with a click of his fingers, he was gone.

'Well', said Jake, 'if that isn't magic, I don't know what is!'

The flutters began fluttering and the children began to fly slowly up the cliff, Millie holding Charlie's hand. One of his flutters had always been slightly smaller than the other which made him fly in circles. He loved this, of course.

In a thrice, the children had reached the top of the cliff and the flutters disappeared, as if by magic. Which of course, it was.

There was Professor Spellbinder to welcome them and in his hand he held a very large key.

'Where are we going now?' asked Sam.

'To school of course. How do you expect to learn magic without going to school? 'the professor replied, as he led them to the old wooden schoolhouse.

He inserted the large key into a large lock. The lock turned rustily and the door creaked, slowly open.

'No one has visited this schoolroom since your grandad came here as a child,' he said.

The children filed in and stared around. The walls were lined with ancient, dusty books all higgledy-piggledy on the shelves.

'He's a bit untidy,' whispered Daisy to her brother.

'Not as untidy as you,' he whispered back.

'I heard that!' said the professor. 'You don't have to be tidy to know magic.'

'Thank goodness for that,' said Daisy, whose
bedroom was always in a mess.

'Now sit down and put your listening ears on,' said
the professor.

'What are they?' asked Freya.

'They are your usual ears but what you will hear today will
be stored in your head until you are ready to give magic back.
When this lesson ends you will not remember anything I have
taught you but when the time comes to share magic with your
grandchildren, you will remember everything.'

'Charlie is only in primary school,' said Millie, 'he may not be
able to learn as much as we can.'

'As I said, it will make not a jot of difference,' replied the
professor, 'he will be just as good as the rest of you when the time
comes. Now sit down at your desks and the lesson will begin.'

The children sat and listened for hours, each feeling as if they were in a kind of dream. Strange shapes and pictures tumbled around them and they heard words in other languages and sounds unlike any other they had heard before. The professor's voice echoed around them, filling their minds with all the magic of heaven and earth. The children were not aware of time: they only knew that at one point the shapes, pictures and sounds grew fainter and fainter until they were gone altogether and they heard the professor's voice loud and clear.

'Well that's that!' he said. 'I've taught you everything I know and it's time you left the island. But first, I must hand each of you a certificate saying that you have been to the Far, Far Distant Land and that I, Professor Spellbinder, have taught you all there is to know about magic. Each of you now is a Master of Magic!'

One by one the children lined up to shake the professor's hand and receive their certificate.

'Now it's getting dark and you must begin your journey back,' he said.

'Is the boat waiting for us?' asked Millie.

'No,' he answered. 'The boat will be full of other passengers. If you remember, you have made promises to the dolphin, the mermaids and the whales so they can fulfil their dreams.'

'Well, we'll have to get back another way,' said Jake, 'and we certainly can't swim that far, especially over the Evil Sea.'

'Well, follow me outside,' said the professor. 'I think you will see I have made other arrangements.'

The children filed out and the professor locked the school room door behind them.

'I don't see anything here that might get us back,' said Sam.

'Well, perhaps a last bit of magic is needed', said the professor and with a click of his fingers, eleven pairs of shining gold flutters, glinting in the moonlight, floated down before them.

'Our flutters have never been made of gold before,' said George.

'They are specially made for long journeys,' said the professor.

'Now, put them on and you will be ready to go. I have had a very happy time with you all and I'm looking forward to seeing your grandchildren, when the time comes. Thank your grandfather for sending you here.'

And with another click of his fingers the flutters lifted them up into the air.

'Thank you, professor!' they shouted. 'We'll never forget this magic day.'

'Yes, you will,' murmured the professor, knowing that they would remember nothing until they had their own grandchildren.

The children hovered in the air, turned round once, waved to the professor and were gone over the harbour and away out to sea. The moon shone brightly, lighting up the water below.

They passed over the Evil Sea and saw again the lovely colours of the jellyfish. They saw the mermaids' rock glowing green from the lights of the Glowfish. They passed over the Dolphins' large

rock and saw eight lanterns shining in the night. They knew then that the octopus was on duty to warn the sailors of danger.

On they flew, night turning into day and the children began to feel very, very sleepy. The flutters carried them onward while they slept.

They were awakened by Grandad saying, 'Old Joe and I have got ice creams for you all!'

The children looked around. They were on the jetty. The flutters were gone, the model boat rocked gently on the waves and they were wearing their normal clothes again.

'It's almost time for us to go home. Your grandmother will have lunch ready by now,' said Grandad.

Ben looked at his watch again. 'It's 12:46,' he said, 'it's only a minute since I last looked!'

'But that's not possible,' said Sam, 'we've been to the Far, Far Distant Land, and met the dolphin, mermaid and whales on the way!'

'We also crossed the Evil Sea,' said Ben.

One by one the children told their grandfather of their adventure and he didn't seem the least bit surprised.

'We met Professor Spellbinder and he said to thank you for sending us, 'said Millie.

'And we went to school and we … that's funny, I can't seem to remember what we learned,' said Mollie and looked rather puzzled. She usually had a very good memory, but none of the others could remember either.

'I do remember the professor shook hands with us and we got the certificates saying we … what did he say?' asked Bea.

'That we are Masters of Magic,' said George, who also had a good memory.

'And we had special gold flutters,' said Charlie, 'to fly us back.'

'It's really strange that none of us can remember what we learned in school,' said Jake, who liked to work things out in his mind.

'You will remember one of these days, I promise you,' said Grandad. 'Right, on to the bus all of you. Old Joe is waiting to drive you back.'

He noticed that young Joe raced ahead of the others and smiled to himself.

'Well, it's good to know I've still got the magic touch,' he thought as he carefully picked the model boat out of the water and followed his grandchildren onto the bus.

The Oxford Children's Hospital is a very special place indeed. Built around the needs of children and their families, with all the clinical areas grouped together under one roof, it is bright and happy with indoor and outdoor play areas, sensory rooms and even a school.

What you may not know is that there wouldn't be a children's hospital in Oxford without charitable support.

Close to £15 million was raised to help create this very special place, and today donations continue to transform the care they are able to offer our young patients.

Sponsored by:

Oxford Children's Hospital Charity would like to say thank you to everyone involved in the magic of this story.

Your generous support helps make the Children's Hospital the best place it can be for the 60,000 children that are treated there each year. From funding cutting-edge VR headsets for the hospital school to toys and games for the playrooms, your kindness helps to transform care across the Oxford Children's Hospital.

You can read more about the impact of your donations at: www.hospitalcharity.co.uk.

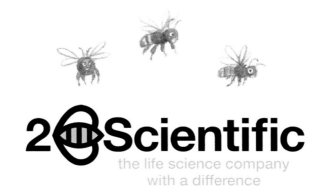

2Scientific
the life science company
with a difference

All proceeds from the sale of this book will go to the
Oxford Children's Hospital Charity

All the books in this series:

The Elephant and
the Angry Farmer

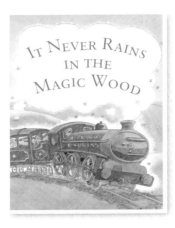

It Never Rains in
the Magic Wood

Grandad's
Magic Shed

The Far, Far
Distant Land

To purchase other books in the series, please visit our website
grandadstories.co.uk